MYTH
RAIDERS

BY A. J. HUNTER

Myth Raiders: Medusa's Curse
Myth Raiders: Claw of the Sphinx

MYTH
RAIDERS

CLAW OF
THE SPHINX

A. J. HUNTER

ILLUSTRATED BY JAMES DE LA RUE

LITTLE, BROWN BOOKS FOR YOUNG READERS
www.lbkids.co.uk

LITTLE, BROWN BOOKS FOR YOUNG READERS

First published in Great Britain in 2016 by Hodder and Stoughton

1 3 5 7 9 10 8 6 4 2

A CIP catalogue record for this book
is available from the British Library.

ISBN 978-0-349-12434-6

Printed and bound in Great Britain by
Clays Ltd, St Ives plc

The paper and board used in this book are made
from wood from responsible sources.

MIX
Paper from
responsible sources
FSC® C104740

Little, Brown Books for Young Readers
An imprint of
Hachette Children's Group
Part of Hodder and Stoughton
Carmelite House
50 Victoria Embankment
London EC4Y 0DZ

An Hachette UK Company
www.hachette.co.uk

www.hachettechildrens.co.uk

CONTENTS

ENCOUNTER WITH
THE TERRIBLE ONE

"Trey, watch out!"

Cold spray crashed into Trey's face in the darkness. He could barely hear his cousin Sam's shouted warning over the cacophony of turbulent water, creaking timbers and fearful cries. An ear-splitting roar rang out above their heads. He felt his legs wobble as the ground beneath him tipped. He braced himself to yell over the noise:

"Sam? Have you got the disc?"

Sam shouted something back at him, but her voice was drowned out. A body bumped into Trey and sent him stumbling backwards. He fell over coils of rope. The wooden floor lurched again, and more water slapped him in the face.

He spluttered, his blurred vision gradually beginning to clear.

A boat. They were on a boat.

Have we actually landed in . . . the Nile? Trey wondered.

Voices rose in terror all around him.

"Abu al-Haul! Abu al-Haul! The gods save us!"

Trey saw shadowy figures in white wraps fall to their knees on the boat, throwing their arms up as if to defend themselves.

Grrraaaaarrrrrrhhhhh!

Trey flinched as another long, shivering roar boomed down out of the starry sky. He felt hot breath on his face. There was a strange, powerful animal smell. He heard the beating of huge wings, the rush of musty air flattening his hair.

A huge shape swept low across the sky, blocking the starlight.

Trey felt something – a figure – stumble over his legs.

"Ow! What the heck?"

"Sam? Is that you?" A hand dragged him close. He could just make out his cousin's blonde hair plastered over her forehead, her eyes like blue diamonds in the darkness.

"What's Michael got us into this time?" she yelled.

"Where's the Heart of Light?" Trey shouted back. They could talk about the Lord of the Light some other time!

"In the backpa—"

Another huge roar cut her off. Above them rose something with the wingspan of a light aeroplane. But it wasn't a bird. *No way* was it a bird.

As it soared above the boat, Trey caught a nightmarish glimpse of an almost human face – narrow and long and covered in a fine film of tawny fur. The mouth was massive, stretched open to show long tapering fangs. Lion fangs. A deep red throat pulsated as the thing let out another roar. The eyes were yellow, huge as moons, brimming with inhuman light.

Claws unsheathed from a paw that was wider than Trey's chest. He rolled aside as they raked the bottom of the boat. Water spurted up between ruptured planks as Trey, Sam and the others gathered in groups at the bow and stern.

The creature circled high, then turned in a long loop and plunged back down towards them.

"Here it comes again," said Sam, scrambling to her feet. "I'm going to give it something to think about." She had a weapon in her hands. A pole or a spear.

"No!" Trey shouted. "You'll get yourself killed!" He couldn't tell whether his cousin had heard.

People flung themselves over the sides of the boat as it rocked and groaned.

Sam spread her feet, drew her arm back and took aim at the creature. She loosed the shaft into the air and hurled herself on the waterlogged deck.

Trey saw the missile strike the creature's outstretched paw. It let out a howl of anguish and jerked aside, one vast wing skimming Trey's back as it sped into the darkness, knocking him over.

He lifted himself on to his hands and knees, water swirling all around him.

"You got it!" he cried. "I can't believe you made that shot!"

Sam was splashing through water up to her waist. "Thanks, but ... we're sinking!"

A shadow moved above their heads and a moment later Trey saw the small boat's mast come crashing down. Splintered wood filled the air. Something hit him hard behind the knees and buckled his legs, making him stumble backwards. He flailed his arms as he fell over the side of the boat.

There was a cold shock as he hit

the river. Water pushed into his nose, burning in his nostrils. Trey thrashed his arms and legs as he tried to get his bearings.

Trapped in a shroud of water. Ears blocked. An iron band tightened around his chest. Desperate for air.

As Trey sank, the memory of Sam's voice rang in his pounding head.

What's Michael got us into this time?

2

NEW ENGLAND: PREPPING FOR THE MYTHIC TIMES

The day had begun so normally. After breakfast that morning, Trey and Sam had excused themselves to race down to the basement. Jennifer Wilson, Trey's mother, frowned as she cleared the kitchen table. "You two spent all day yesterday down there," she said. "I'd almost think you were up to something."

Trey gave a fake laugh that he hoped didn't sound too nervous. It had been about sixteen hours since he and Sam had returned from Ancient Greece, and the hours were ticking past on day two of their mythic mission.

A meteor shower would hit the earth in three days' time. Except that it wasn't just *any* meteor shower – it was an attack by the Lords of the Dark – and it would smash the whole planet to smithereens unless Trey and Sam could stop it!

How did they know this? Because

Michael, Lord of the Light, had told them so. And Michael was not your average guy.

"You're here!" gasped Sam, staring at Michael.

The first Lord of the Light stood in the middle of the basement floor, as though he had been waiting for them. He adjusted his white cloak, belted at the waist and shining with a sparkling light that matched his beard and long hair. Piercing, silver-grey eyes were set deep in his hawk-like face.

"Greetings, Chosen Ones," he said.

Trey blinked. He could never quite get used to the fact that Michael always looked like he was standing in a strong wind. His hair and beard blew out to one side, his cloak rippling and snapping.

That was because he wasn't from Earth – and he had to move very fast to keep up with the planet as it orbited the sun at 108,000 kilometres per hour.

Michael was holding the two halves of the Heart of Light, an ancient metal disc, one half-circle in each hand. The Heart of Light was the centre of the Warrior's Shield, a powerful weapon against the Dark. But long ago the shield had been broken and its pieces scattered. As the Chosen Ones, Sam and Trey had to find the lost fragments.

Trey could still hardly believe it, but when the two halves of the Heart of Light were united, he and Sam would be sent back through time and across the world in their desperate search.

The broken disc didn't *look* powerful. It was about the size of a small plate, both halves covered all over with intricate engravings. Skulls. Swords. Strange, creepy-looking animals. Whorls and wiggly lines and geometric designs, etched into the greyish metal by an artist who had lived and died hundreds of thousands of years before humans were even supposed to have existed.

"Are you ready for your second task?" Michael asked, his voice deep and low.

Sam was grinning at him. "We're fuelled up with pancakes. I think we're good to go!"

Michael gave a solemn nod. "Your next journey will take you back four and a half thousand years, to the time of the pharaohs."

Trey gasped. "Ancient Egypt? Cool!"

"The creature your people named 'the Sphinx' will hold the key to the discovery of the next fragment of the Warrior's Shield."

Trey saw a puzzled look on Sam's face. He guessed that his cousin was probably thinking the same thing he was.

I thought the Sphinx was just a big stone statue in the middle of a desert?

Or is it?

"Hold on." Trey ran upstairs, ducking past Mrs Wilson on the way to his bedroom. Opening his laptop, he googled "Ancient Egypt" and "Sphinx". Two minutes later, he was back down in the basement, a folded printout photo in his pocket.

Sam was talking to Michael. "Here's the thing," she said as Trey reached the bottom of the stairs. "*Weapons* would be kind of handy. If we'd had a couple of bazookas when we went to Ancient Greece, we'd have saved ourselves a lot of trouble."

Michael looked gravely at her. "Weapons must be earned. Even for the Chosen Ones."

"And outwitting Medusa doesn't count?"

Trey jumped in before Sam could

say anything that might upset the first Lord of the Light. "So, Ancient Egypt, huh? Can you tell us exactly what we need to do when we get there?"

"We go to the Sphinx," said Sam, ticking off on her fingers. "We find out where the second part of the Warrior's Shield is hidden, we grab it – we come home. Simple!"

"The Sphinx is a gigantic statue," Trey said to Sam. "Statues don't generally give much away." He looked at Michael. "Do we have to find an inscription or something?"

"I have told you all that I can," said Michael. "You must walk the path of your destiny alone."

"I hate it when he says things like

that," sighed Sam. "It's the opposite of helpful."

"Sam's right about weapons, though," Trey said. "Shouldn't we be able to defend ourselves – just in case we meet up with something like the harpies that attacked us in Greece?" Just mentioning those hideous winged creatures with their long teeth, claws and rotting flesh made his skin crawl.

"If you follow the true path and surrender yourself to your fate, you shall find Weapons of Light," Michael said. "They await your hands."

"Cool!" breathed Sam. "When you say 'Weapons of Light', do you mean, like . . . fiery swords?" She mimed some sweeping moves, while making sounds that Trey guessed were meant to be rippling flames.

He rolled his eyes. His English cousin was the perfect person to have by his side in a tight spot, but she could also be a bit of a loon.

"We should get going," he told her.

Trey and Sam each took a half of the disc from Michael's outstretched hands.

Sam's eyes shone. "Ready?" she asked.

Trey nodded, swallowing hard. Nervous and excited at the same time. "Ready," he agreed. "On three. One ... two ... "

Sam slammed her half of the Heart of Light into his. "Three!"

3

SPHINX? WHAT SPHINX?

Sam plunged into cold water, kicking out and swimming strongly as she looked around in the darkness, desperately trying to get her bearings. *Where's Trey?* She couldn't see him anywhere. The small boat had disintegrated under her, but she'd managed to swim free of the debris. Her eyes adjusted to the gloom, and she was able to pick out a few details.

She was in a river, and she could see a sandy bank on her right. The flying, roaring, clawing thing was nowhere to be seen or heard.

Where was Trey? The last she'd seen of him was when he'd fallen backwards off the boat. So much had already happened since the disc had brought them here – and they weren't even on dry land yet.

She could hear the sound of people splashing their way to the shore.

A gush of water erupted off to her left, followed by floundering noises and panicky gasping. A pale face emerged from the gloom, and she struck out towards it. "Trey! Are you OK?"

"Yes," he gurgled, spitting water. "Kind of."

"Come on, then!" She powered to the shore, Trey doggy-paddling in her wake.

A frightened voice caught her attention: "Amsu! Amsu!"

Amsu?

"Amsu! My son! He cannot swim!"

"Get yourself to shore, Trey," Sam said. "I won't be a minute."

"Be careful!" Trey gasped, as Sam turned and swam back into the deep belly of the river.

She saw a spurt of white water. A thin arm reaching up.

Gotcha!

She swam fast, coming up under the boy. Sam turned on to her back, cupped his chin in her hand, and kicked out for the bank with him thrashing away on top of her.

"Abu al-Haul!" he wailed. "The Terrible One!"

"Calm down!" she told him. "You'll be fine."

The little boy became quiet, lying limp in the water as she towed him ashore.

She lowered her legs and felt sand between her toes. She straightened up, holding the boy in her arms. She heaved him up the bank and on to dry land, her arms shaking.

A man fell to his knees beside the boy.

"Amsu? Speak to me!" he cried.

"Papa?" The boy's eyes opened weakly. He reached out and the man gathered him into his arms.

"Thank you," he said to Sam, clinging to the boy. "You saved his life!"

"You're welcome," said Sam, squeezing water out of her clothes. She saw Trey walking soggily towards her.

"What was that thing that attacked you?" he asked the man.

The stranger's face paled. "A nightmare come true," he said, his voice filled with horror. "Abu al-Haul. The Terrible One. I never believed that the old stories could be real. But we should praise the gods for our preservation." Then he looked at Sam and Trey, frowning slightly. "I do not recognise your faces. Who are you?"

Sam gave Trey a swift glance. "If you take us somewhere to dry off, we'll tell you all about it."

The man led them to a small village close to the river. As they walked, he told them his name was Haji. They bid a quick goodbye to the other men who had been on the wrecked boat, each of them breaking off from the group and staggering into the deep dark of night, eager to get home.

Haji ushered them into a small, single-storey mud-brick house in the middle of the village. The single-roomed building had rough brown walls and a floor of hard-packed earth. The slightly smoky air smelt of burning animal fat from two small lamps that stood on a shelf. There wasn't much in the way of furniture. Some simple stools. Reed mats.

Haji's son, Amsu, and a couple of other

children watched Sam and Trey with wide, fascinated eyes. A woman in a long white dress ladled out bowls of vegetable stew from a cooking pot and handed it to them. She listened, open-mouthed, to her husband's account of the attack.

"It cannot be true," she kept saying, shaking her head, her long black hair swinging. "Is the drought not harsh enough, that demons are sent to trouble us also? Why are the gods being so cruel?"

"There's a drought?" asked Trey.

"For two seasons now, the river has failed to rise," Haji said mournfully. He gestured to his wife. "Suhad does what she can with our dwindling food supplies, and our beloved pharaoh is

emptying his own storerooms of food to help keep us alive ... but if the blessed Nile fails us again this season, all will be lost." He grimaced, bowing his head. "And now our fishing boat is gone, and with it any hope of catching enough fish to feed my family."

Sam had learnt at school that most of the people in Ancient Egypt lived along the banks of the Nile and relied on the annual floods to survive.

"Why would the gods set monsters upon us?" asked Suhad. "Have we been wicked? How have we offended them?"

"I'm not sure it works like that," said Sam. She looked at them. "What *was* that flying thing? I heard people yelling something. *Aboo* . . . ?"

"Abu al-Haul," said Haji with a shudder. "The Terrible One."

Sam caught Trey's eye, and guessed he was having the same thought as her. "The Terrible One" sounded like a good name for a creature guarding a piece of the Warrior's Shield.

Which we need to hurry up and start looking for . . .

"Where do you children come from, with your strange clothing?" Suhad asked. The woman was looking at Sam and Trey with a curious expression on her face. She turned to her husband. "The girl has yellow hair. It is not natural!"

"It *is* natural where we come from," Sam said quickly.

"We've come here to find the Sphinx," said Trey, before the woman could ask too many questions. "You know . . . the Great Sphinx?" he added. "The statue? At Giza?"

"Where the pyramids are," Sam continued helpfully. "You can't miss it."

"The ... great ... *Sphinx* ...?" said Haji, shaking his head.

"Don't tell us we've come to the wrong place," said Sam. "Are we *anywhere* near Giza?"

"The great works at Giza are very close by," said Haji. "Khafre's pyramid is under construction and they say it will be finished in only five seasons. But I know of no statue – save those in the temples. And none is called ... 'Sphinx'."

"OK, this is weird," Trey muttered. Sam nodded in agreement.

"If no one's heard of the Sphinx," she said, "we must be in, like, *Ancient-*Ancient Egypt."

"It is late," said Haji. "You must sleep

here for the night. Our home is your home – it's the least we can do." He gestured towards woven mats that lay against the wall. Suhad was already busy tucking the children in under light blankets.

The cousins looked at each other. "I *am* kind of tired," said Trey.

Sam nodded. "That would be great, thank you," she said, taking a blanket from Haji. They'd rest now and in the morning ...

We'll try to find what happened to the Sphinx!

4

THE PYRAMIDS

"Well, they weren't kidding us," Trey said, gazing across the desert. "There's definitely no Great Sphinx here."

"I can see that," breathed Sam. "But ... wow ... *look* at this place!"

Trey shielded his eyes against the blazing hot morning sun. Shadows reached out across the stony landscape that spilled down from the sandy ridge they were standing on. Long, low mud-brick houses stretched away from them, set in long geometric lines and teeming with people. And beyond them ...

"Pyramids," Trey gasped. "Actual, just-built pyramids!"

Two were finished, towering above the world, sheathed in smooth white stone that dazzlingly reflected the sunlight. A third pyramid was still being built. Long winding ramps led up to its jagged upper edge, and lines of men dragged a huge stone block up the long slope, while others dropped rollers in front to help with the immense task of moving the stone.

Trey pointed at a long, solitary stone outcrop that blocked the way between them and the half-built pyramid. He was starting to understand what had happened. "See that?"

"Yes," said Sam. "So what?"

"That's where the Great Sphinx *should* be," Trey said, remembering his printed-out picture of the statue.

Sam blinked. "Oh, I get it," she said. "They haven't carved it out yet." She shook her head. "So ... Michael has sent us back too far in time?" She turned to look at him. "How are we going to use the Sphinx to help us find the piece of the Warrior's Shield when the Sphinx doesn't even exist yet?"

"The statue may not exist," Trey said. "But I've got a feeling the Sphinx does. I got a glimpse of that thing that attacked us last night. It had a human face – well, kind of *half*-human, half-lion." Sam gave him a curious look. "Wings, but not a bird. Massive paws with killer claws." He raised an eyebrow. "Ring any bells?"

"You mean it was an actual *sphinx*?" Sam said. "But the statue doesn't have wings."

"Statues and pictures of Egyptian sphinxes aren't winged," Trey agreed. "But Persian ones are, and so are Greek ones. What if the Egyptians just left the wings off for some reason?"

Sam let out a long, low whistle. "So,

Abu al-Haul is a sphinx ... a *real-life* sphinx."

"You're funny." They spun at the sudden voice behind them.

"Hey, Amsu ... Where'd you spring from?" Sam gasped as they stared at the little boy standing behind them.

"I followed you," Amsu said. "You talk about strange things." He eyed them thoughtfully. "In the stories my mother tells me, Abu al-Haul is the guardian of a hidden treasure. Is that what you're looking for?"

"If we were, would you know where we'd find it?" Trey asked carefully. Could the Warrior's Shield be among this hidden treasure?

"No," Amsu said. "But my father used

to work for a man who might know. Ardeth Bey – a great scholar." He nodded. "You should speak to him. He lives in the south. In the city of Memphis."

"How far is it?" Trey asked.

The boy shrugged. "By camel, it would take you, maybe ... " He frowned. "A quarter of a day. Less on a fast camel."

"Can you help us find a fast camel?" Sam said.

Amsu's face broke into a grin. "Of course!"

"Ow!" groaned Sam, rubbing her backside. "Who knew camels were so lumpy? And what a pong!"

Perched so far above the ground, and

being flung from side to side by his camel's swaying walk, Trey was feeling a bit seasick.

To one side of them, boats moved across the silvery face of the river. Occasionally, Trey spotted long brown humps in the water. At first he thought they must be sandbanks or floating logs – until one of them opened a cavernous mouth in a long yawn. They were ...

"Hippos!" Sam cried, laughing out loud.

Fortunately for Trey's queasy stomach, they'd reached the outskirts of Memphis. Jostling people filled the busy harbours and the narrow streets of mud-brick houses. In the distance, Trey could see stone temples and palaces. They'd been

given directions to Ardeth Bey's house –
turn right at the red palace, left at the
vegetable stall – and now they arrived at
a white two-storey building halfway up
a hill on the edge of the city.

Sam slid from her saddle, wincing as
she stretched her limbs. Trey dropped
down to the ground beside her, easing

his aching muscles. They tied the camels up, then climbed a set of steps to an arched doorway. There were hieroglyphs painted on the wall next to the door.

"You know all about history and stuff," Sam said. "Can you read this?"

Trey peered at the neatly painted little images. "A hand, a bird, a foot and a kind of oval shape that looks like an open mouth," he said, nodding. "It says, 'Knock three times and ask for Ardeth Bey.'"

Sam stared at him. "*Seriously?*"

"Of course not," said Trey. "What am I – hieroglyphic guy? It could say, 'No junk mail,' for all I know." He stepped up to the door and knocked.

They waited.

"Maybe no one's home?" said Sam.

Trey lifted his fist to knock again, just as the door swung open. He stared at the tall figure that stood in the doorway.

"We're really sorry to disturb you," Trey began. "We're—"

"You are the Chosen Ones," the man interrupted, turning and walking away down the hallway. He paused and looked back at them, as though surprised that they weren't following him. "I have been expecting you."

5

A ROYAL INTERVENTION

S am and Trey stepped over the threshold. "You were *expecting* us?" Sam asked.

"Indeed," said Ardeth Bey. "I have awaited your coming for many years." He pointed to her forehead. "You bear the mark of Light, the sign I have been looking for."

Sam's fingers came up to the scar a harpy's claw had given her. "Wow," she breathed. "You know what it is?"

"Of course." Ardeth Bey stepped into a room. "Welcome to my home."

Sam could see immediately that this was a more upmarket place than the one they had spent the night in. The walls were smooth and white, hung with brightly patterned fabrics and decorated with painted pictures of people with animal heads.

"So," said Trey, "if you've been expecting us, does that mean you're a Lord of the Light?"

Ardeth Bey shook his head. "I am but a vessel that the Light fills." He stopped, turning suddenly, staring at them with haunted eyes. "There are others," he said sharply. "Agents of the Dark. Beware. You will not know them until they strike. They are deadly—"

"Ardeth Bey!" called a girl's voice from a room ahead of them. "I'm bored now. Whoever your visitors are, tell them to go away, or I shall have their heads exhibited on spikes in my father's palace!"

The girl appeared at the end of the hallway, fists on hips.

Sam guessed she was a little younger than them, very tall and thin with a long, slender face and huge black eyes. Her hair was cut square across her forehead and hung straight to her shoulders, smooth and black and shiny.

Her body was sheathed in a tight dress patterned in red and white. There was a loose white shawl around her shoulders.

She stared at Sam and Trey.

"Princess, behave yourself," Ardeth Bey said. "These guests have travelled far to see me. Show them some courtesy."

The princess stepped forward, her chin raised. "Welcome, travellers from afar," she said. "I am Shepsetkau, daughter of the mighty Khafre, Pharaoh of Upper and Lower Egypt, conqueror of the Canaanites and the Nubians, son of Khufu, builder of the greatest wonder of the modern world." She waved a hand. "You need not prostrate yourselves."

"I wasn't going to," said Sam, trying not to laugh. "What did you say your name was?"

"Princess Shepsetkau, third daughter of our lord Khafre," said Ardeth Bey. "She honours me by coming to my house for lessons in reading and writing."

"My father does not approve of his daughters learning the skills of a scribe," said Shepsetkau. "So I come secretly when I can get away from the palace unseen."

Sam looked at Trey, who was gazing at the princess with saucer-eyes. "She's a princess," she said. "How cool is that?"

"Very cool," mumbled Trey.

The princess frowned. "What is this 'cool'?"

"It means great," said Sam. "Marvellous. Wonderful. Brilliant."

Shepsetkau inclined her head. "Then it is most *cool* to meet you," she said.

"Can we call you Sheppie?" asked Sam. "Your name is a bit of a mouthful."

Shepsetkau hesitated, and then nodded. "You may."

Ardeth Bey showed Trey and Sam to comfortable seats, then sat down himself and regarded them with deep, dark eyes. The princess stood behind him, watching them with aloof interest.

"What are your names, Chosen Ones?" asked Ardeth Bey.

"I'm Sam and this is my cousin, Trey," Sam began. "We're here to find part of the Warrior's Shield."

"I have read of the shield," said Ardeth Bey. "It is part of the lost Armour of the Light. But there are no scripts that tell where it might be found."

"OK," said Sam. "In that case, question one: do you know what a sphinx is?"

"I do not," said Ardeth Bey.

"Well, the thing is, I think we met one last night," Sam continued. "It attacked a fishing boat near here. It's a weird-looking thing. Face of a human, body of a lion ... "

"It looks a bit like this," said Trey suddenly. He took out a water-stained piece of paper from his shirt pocket. He handed it to Ardeth Bey. The princess leaned forward, her eyes wide.

"It's a picture of the Great Sphinx," Trey whispered to Sam. "I got it off the internet just before we left. I thought it might help."

Clever!

"Except the sphinx we met had wings," Sam explained. "Huge wings."

"And it wasn't anything like as big as the one in the picture," added Trey. "And it didn't have a headdress. And its nose wasn't missing."

"Why are the great pyramids in such disrepair?" asked the princess, frowning at the image.

"Because this is a depiction of a possible far-off *future*, Princess," said Ardeth Bey. He nodded. "The creature resembles the old tales of Abu al-Haul."

"That's what everyone else has been calling it," agreed Trey. "They thought it wasn't real ... until it attacked them. We need to find it. We were told you might be able to help."

Ardeth Bey's brow wrinkled. "Why did it leave its guardianship of the tomb?" he muttered to himself. He looked up at the cousins. "Abu al-Haul never leaves the tomb." He started to stand, moving stiffly, and the princess bent to help. "I need to show you something," he said. "And I must tell you the tale of Horos-Aha."

6

THE CHILDREN
OF HOROS

Ardeth Bey led them through cool, beautifully decorated rooms to an arched doorway that took them to an external stone stairway up on to the flat roof. From here, they could see the line of baked brown cliffs that ran alongside the road from Giza. The cliffs dipped to reveal the desert beyond.

Ardeth Bey pointed. "Look to the horizon," he said. "Can you see two hills?"

Sam squinted into the distance.

Yes. Way, way off. Two ridges against the sky.

"Between those two hills lies the lost tomb of Horos-Aha," said Ardeth Bey.

"I didn't know that," murmured the princess. "I have been told of Horos-Aha. He was the son of Pharaoh Narmer who first unified the two kingdoms many lifetimes ago." She looked at Ardeth Bey. "Why is the location of his tomb kept secret?" she asked.

"Because legends tell of a great evil that lurks at the door to the tomb, protecting its treasures," Ardeth Bey replied. "In the days of your father's father's father, people would venture deep into the desert, in search of the tomb." He shook his head. "None ever returned."

"Do you know what *kind* of great evil it is?" asked Trey.

"Abu al-Haul," intoned Ardeth Bey solemnly. "The Terrible One. A creature with the body of a lion, the wings of an eagle and the head of a man."

He shook his head. "Why he left his post and came to the Nile, I can only guess. Perhaps thirst drove him? The long drought has dried many desert wells."

"We totally need to go and check out that tomb," said Sam. "I bet that's where we'll find the piece of the Warrior's Shield."

The princess smiled. "The three of us will seek Horos-Aha's tomb!"

"Hold on," said Sam uneasily. "I don't think we can take you with us."

Sheppie lifted an eyebrow. "You shall not *take* me," she said. "I shall allow you to *accompany* me. I am the third daughter of Khafre, and my will is law throughout the land! Besides, I'm bored. I want an adventure. Trust me. I can help. I will get horses."

She raced out of the doorway. Ardeth

Bey shook his head as he watched her disappear.

"The princess is strong willed," he said in a sorrowful voice.

Trey grinned at Sam. "She reminds me of someone . . ."

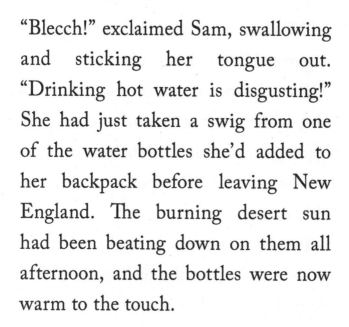

"Blecch!" exclaimed Sam, swallowing and sticking her tongue out. "Drinking hot water is disgusting!" She had just taken a swig from one of the water bottles she'd added to her backpack before leaving New England. The burning desert sun had been beating down on them all afternoon, and the bottles were now warm to the touch.

Ahead of them, the cliffs loomed ominously, sharp-edged against the sky and torn apart by deep cracks and crevices.

"That seems the best way in," said Trey, pointing to a long canyon that wound between the shoulders of jagged rock.

"Keep your eyes open," Sam warned. "We mustn't let the Sphinx see us."

"Maybe we should dismount?" suggested Trey. "Keep a low profile?"

They climbed down from their horses and made their way into the canyon, leading the animals by their reins, Trey in the middle, Sheppie and Sam on either side.

The back of Sam's neck began to prickle – she had the feeling they were being watched. But apart from the thud of their horses' hooves in the sand, and the snort of their breath, the entire world was silent . . .

Crack! A sharp noise made her snap her head around. A dark fissure ran down a sheer wall of stone.

Sam stared, her pulse hammering. Their horses whinnied in fear, stamping and pulling on their reins.

The crack was widening.

Two doors! Two huge rough-hewn doors were opening outwards from the cliff face.

"Isis protect us," gasped Sheppie.

The massive doorway yawned like a black throat.

"Is that the tomb?" murmured Trey, his voice shaking, his face grey.

Before Sam could answer, her horse reared, almost dragging her off her feet. As she struggled to stay upright, she heard a rhythmic rumble from within the deep darkness of the cave. She knew what the sound was.

Hooves!

"Watch out!" she gasped to the others, as a group of riders burst out of the cave, clouds of dust billowing around them. The riders hurtled towards them, filling the air with weird, uncanny animal cries.

Sam just managed to twist her hand free of the reins as her horse bolted.

Sheppie let out a cry of fear, stumbling backwards as the riders pounded forward.

Sam was vaguely aware of their three horses galloping away.

The screams of the oncoming riders turned her blood to ice.

Inhuman! Totally inhuman!

The riders pulled their horses to a halt, swivelling inwards to surround the cousins and the princess. Sam's vision was filled with horses' legs and kicked-up sand, the faces of their new captors obscured by the fierce sun.

Trey threw his arms up. "We surrender," he shouted.

Sam lifted her arms. Sheppie fell to her knees, folding herself up and touching her forehead to the ground, muttering prayers.

The horses moved closer. The riders'

faces were still in shadow, but Sam saw they were wearing sleeveless jerkins and short kilts of overlapping strips of brown leather. Wide bands of bronze circled their forearms and calves, matching the heavy collars on their shoulders. Each of them carried a long spear with a leaf-shaped head.

Sam turned to the nearest rider, squinting against the dazzling sunlight.

"You leave us alone!" she shouted. "We're the Chos ... " Her voice died as the rider threw his head back and let out an animal howl.

The dust cleared to reveal his terrible face and Trey's eyes grew wide with fear. "He's ... he's ... "

"A jackal," Sam gasped in horror. "We are in so much trouble."

The lead rider's open jaws were lined with slavering fangs. Beside him was a man with a hawk-head dominated by savage, pitiless eyes over a razor-sharp beak. There were also horned ram heads, yellow-eyed panther heads, grinning baboon heads, gaping crocodile heads – all of them mad-eyed and snarling.

Sam gagged at the smell that came from them. It was like a toxic mix of rotting meat and sour milk and open sewers.

A hawk-headed rider lifted his spear, aiming its point at the three captives.

"Bow before the Children of Horos,

accursed ones!" His voice was shrill and harsh. "None may disturb the long sleep of Horos-Aha."

White lightning ran down the length of the spear, setting the head alight with an intense blue flame.

"All who come here must die!"

7

THE WEAPONS OF THE CHOSEN ONES

The voices of the other riders rose, baying and growling and yelping and howling as the terrifying creature drew back his arm and let the spear fly.

It was heading straight for Trey!

Sam flung herself at her cousin,

tackling him to the ground a fraction of a second before the burning spear buried itself deep into the sand.

She scrambled back up, grabbing at the spear shaft.

"Oww!" The shaft seared her flesh like hot metal. She snatched her fingers away. Other animal-headed riders were aiming their spears, their yells rising.

A high voice cut through the hideous noise. "Hear me, Children of Horos!"

Sam swung around. Sheppie was on her feet again, her arms stretched out, a defiant light in her eyes. "I am Shepsetkau," she cried as the animal noises died away. "Third daughter of Khafre, son of Khutu, son of Sneteru, son of Huni, known as the well-remembered . . ."

Sam's head began to spin as Sheppie listed more and more names, the animal-headed riders watching her in strange silence as she spoke.

". . . son of Merneith, son of Djet . . . son of Horos-Aha!"

There were a few snorts and growls from the riders as they stared at her with their uncanny, inhuman eyes. Only Sam was close enough to see how Sheppie's outstretched hands trembled. One by one, the creatures lowered their spears but none put their weapons away.

"I can trace my lineage back to your dark master!" Sheppie continued.

"Bow down before me and obey my commands."

The hawk-headed rider who had thrown the spear climbed down from his horse and strode forward, towering two heads higher than Sheppie.

Wow! thought Sam. *This is totally going to work! Way to go, Sheppie!*

His hooked beak opened, eyes glittering. "None but Horos-Aha may command us," he croaked, lifting a claw-like hand and bringing it down heavily on Sheppie's shoulder. She winced and cried out, driven to her knees.

"You shall be sacrificed to the glory of our master!" the monstrous rider roared. He dug his claws into her shoulder and wrenched her up on to her feet. "When the sun drops below the horizon, you three shall die on the altar of the Temple of Horos-Aha!" His voice rose to a shriek. "Take them away!"

Six of the hideous riders jumped down and moved towards Sam and Trey. Sam braced herself, lifting her arms, fists balled. She saw Trey try to duck between two of them. A heavy blow sent him sprawling to the sand. A booted foot came down on his back, pinning him there. Sam lunged to aid her cousin, but had to rear back as a crocodile head snapped at her, with teeth like jagged glass.

Hands caught her from behind and

she was lifted off her feet. She kicked out, struggling wildly. A hand closed over her mouth, and arms tightened around her chest, squeezing the breath out of her.

She was flung face down over the back of one of the horses. A rider mounted, one hand holding her down, claws like knives in the small of her back. So painful! So hard to breathe!

The riders turned to the gaping entrance in the cliff, riding two abreast into the cold darkness. Trey was draped over another horse just ahead. Sam couldn't see Sheppie.

The doors closed with an echoing boom. As the sound faded, Sam realised that their chances of finding the next piece of the Warrior's Shield had also faded to nothing.

"Anyone got any brilliant ideas for how we get out of here?" Sam asked, pacing restlessly up and down. "And is this a good time to mention I'm just the tiniest bit claustrophobic?"

The dreadful animal-headed creatures had thrown them into a small room and slammed a heavy door on them. A long narrow shaft in the ceiling let in a small amount of sunlight – just enough to see one another. The room had been hacked out of the solid rock. There was rubble strewn over the uneven floor, and rags and other stuff piled in corners.

"What *were* those things?" Trey wondered aloud. "And how come Ardeth Bey didn't warn us to watch out for them?"

"How should I know?" snapped Sam, her voice rising as she quickened her pace, pressing her hands against the walls as if trying to push through them and get out.

Trey had the uncomfortable feeling his cousin was beginning to panic a bit.

Sheppie was sitting cross-legged on the floor, her back straight, her hands on her knees and her eyes closed. She hadn't moved or spoken since they had been dumped in here. Trey guessed she was probably praying really hard to Isis or another of her protective gods.

Let's hope Isis isn't too busy to listen!

"Did you know the Ancient Egyptians

carved out places like this with just copper chisels and wooden mallets?" Trey said, hoping to take Sam's mind off her fear of small spaces. "And all they had to see with were little lamps fuelled with olive oil. They put salt in the oil to make the flame burn more pure. Isn't that interesting?"

Sam stared at him. "We're about to get eaten alive by a bunch of animal-headed freaks, and you're giving me a *history lesson*?" she said. "Reality check, Trey! We need to get out of here!"

"I was just *saying*," muttered Trey. "I wanted to take your mind off ..." he gestured around them, "... *this*." He got up and listlessly kicked a small stone across the floor. It hit one of the piles of cloth with a dull clang.

Weird ...

Frowning, he went to investigate, crouching and lifting the rags.

"Wow!" he said. "Take a look at these!"

Wrapped in the cloth were several chisels and some battered old wooden mallets. "They must have been left behind when the work was finished." He picked up a chisel and grabbed a mallet by its handle.

"This could be our way out of here," Sam said, brightening. She took another chisel and jammed the point into a crack that ran down the wall. Then she gave it a hefty whack with a mallet. She jumped back as a whole chunk of the wall broke off and fell to the ground with a low clatter.

Trey stared in amazement. The crack seemed to go right through the wall – and there was a chink of light from the deepest part.

He put his eye to the crack. "It's another room," he said. "Sam – you're a total genius! Another few whacks and we'll be able to get through." Hope and relief flooded through him.

Sam grinned from ear to ear. "I knew that would happen," she said. "It was my big plan all along."

"Isis guided your hand," said Sheppie, who had come up silently behind them. "I prayed for her help, and she heard my words."

"Well, tell Isis we said thanks," said Sam, lifting the mallet and chisel again. "Stand back, guys."

Trey and Sheppie stepped backwards while Sam wielded the tools.

Bam! Bam!

Cra–a–ack!

Another hunk of stone broke free.

A beam of light raked in from a long fissure.

Whack!

More stone crumbled away, revealing a section of a room.

Trey edged through first, with Sam and Sheppie close behind.

This new room had smooth walls, covered from floor to ceiling with the most beautiful, dazzling pictures that Trey had ever seen – brightly coloured depictions of animal-headed creatures like the ones that had captured them. In among the pictures were endless columns of hieroglyphic writing.

Light poured down through wide cracks in the roof. Up above them, Trey could see patches of blue sky. Freedom!

"We can climb out!" said Trey, gesturing to the shafts above them. He looked around the room. There were stone chests against the walls, some laden with small gold statues and ornaments. "If we pile these up we can use them to reach the ceiling."

"Works for me," said Sam, crouching by a chest and digging her fingers under it. "Sheppie? Want to give us a hand lifting this?"

Sheppie didn't reply. She was standing facing the wall, her fingers tracing a column of writing and her lips moving as she read. There was another stone chest at her feet, its lid circled with copper straps.

"What is it?" Sam asked. "Found something interesting?"

"It is an old script," Sheppie said in a strangely quiet voice. "But I can make the words out . . . I *think*."

"What does it say?" asked Trey, joining her at the wall. "'Please do not touch the exhibits'?"

"'In this casket lie the Weapons of Light,'" Sheppie read out. "'Placed here by the mighty priest Imhotep in the reign of the god-king Ka.'" She knitted her brows, as though trying to remember something. "Ka was the grandfather of Horos-Aha. The ancient texts say he loathed his grandson, and banished him for his evil ways."

"I like the sound of this Ka guy," murmured Sam.

"Weapons of Light," said Trey. "Just like Michael said we'd find."

"Wait, there is more to read," said Sheppie. "'May these magical items rest in safety until the Chosen Ones come.'" She swivelled round to Sam and Trey, her eyes bright. "You are the Chosen Ones!"

"Too right we are," said Sam. "Whatever's in that box belongs to us."

She and Trey knelt either side of the chest. They lifted the heavy lid. Sam could feel her muscles trembling with the strain as they gently placed the stone slab on the ground.

"Ohhh ... kayyyy ..." murmured Sam. "That's weird."

Lying in the casket were two sword

hilts – with no blades attached. One was bound with silver wire and had a crescent moon etched into it. The other was wrapped in gold wire and showed a sun with eight pointed rays.

Sam reached in.

She closed her fingers around the silver hilt and picked it up. It had a slightly warm feeling – just like the Heart of Light. "It's got a moon on it – just like my scar," she said, touching her forehead.

Trey took hold of the golden hilt. He held it up. "Does the shape of yours fit your hand perfectly?"

"Yes, it does," said Sam, squeezing the hilt and shaking it. "But ... this can't be *all* there is." She peered into the top of the hilt – where the blade ought to be. "Where's the 'on' button?"

"There are a few final words," said Sheppie, raising her hand. "It reads: 'When the chosen hand chooses a weapon, help will be given.'"

"What does that mean?" said Sam. "'Choose weapon'?"

Shhhhunk!

Sam had to jerk her head back as a sword blade shot out of the hilt, narrowly missing her. She staggered to her feet. "Woah!" she gasped. "That thing almost had my eye out!" She held the sword up, its sharp blade gleaming with silvery light. "It's amazing! I love it!"

Trey held his hilt at arm's length. "Choose weapon ..."

With a flash, a long, metal-shafted

axe burst into existence. "Awesome!" he crowed, lifting the axe high.

Sheppie stared at them, her face awestruck. "You truly are the Chosen Ones," she gasped.

The cousins ran their fingers cautiously over their blades. Both were razor-sharp, the metal shining.

Trey swung the axe around his head, his arm moving with seamless skill as the blade cut through the air. "You know what's *really* awesome?"

Sam made a spinning move with her sword that would have taken three animal heads clean off. "That you know exactly how to use it?" she said with a fierce grin. "It's like the thing is right inside my brain."

Trey nodded. "I only have to think of a move and I can do it."

"So, how about we get out of here?" suggested Sam, pointing her sword up towards the sunlit shaft. "Let's find that lost tomb and get the next piece of the Warrior's Shield. And if that Sphinx feels like sticking his nose in," she added, swinging her sword in a glittering arc, "he's going to get a big surprise!"

8

ABU AL-HAUL

Afternoon was turning into evening when the cousins and Sheppie came to a stop at the edge of a cliff. The sun struck two distant hills, and they glowed with a golden light. But the shadows were deepening.

It had been Trey's idea to walk along

the cliff top. That way, they could spot any attempted ambushes from the Children of Horos or from the Sphinx.

Trey looked at Sam. "Ardeth Bey said the tomb was between these two hills."

"Isn't the Sphinx supposed to be guarding it?" Sam peered down at the smooth stretch of sand that lay between the jutting hills. "I don't see him."

"Maybe he's gone walkabout again?"

"Could thirst have driven him to the Nile once more?" suggested Sheppie.

"Maybe . . ." said Trey uncertainly.

Sam led them down the steep slope, her every nerve tingling, dreading an attack.

As they came to the floor of the canyon, she glanced at Trey. He was gripping his axe in both hands, his face set and pale. She realised she was holding her sword so tightly that her knuckles were white.

They walked across the burning sand. "I think this is actually going to be OK," whispered Trey – half a second before a heavy shadow fell over the group.

Sam swirled round, staring in horror at the Sphinx as he swooped down towards them. His huge body was muscular and leonine, and tawny feathers rippled on his wings. But it was his head that really caught her attention. There was a mass of shaggy brown hair pulled back from a high forehead and sweeping out to either side. The face was long and narrow and strangely beautiful, with large, deep-set eyes and high cheekbones – furry like a cat's face, but with a human nose and mouth.

Sam's eyes were drawn to his forepaws. One was being held at a strange angle. Sam saw a wooden shaft sticking out of the paw, a dark stain on the matted fur.

That's where I hit him with the harpoon. Poor thing – he must be in agony!

The massive creature snarled as he landed. The ground trembled and a great spray of sand filled the air. The Sphinx bounded towards them, lips drawn back from gaping fangs. Sam took a step backwards, holding her sword up in her trembling hand, her mouth desert-dry with fear.

"All who dare to approach the tomb of Horos-Aha must die!" the Sphinx bellowed, his voice as loud and deep as a thunder-crack, his breath like a hot wind. He raised a paw and swiped at them with razor-sharp claws.

Sam darted in front of Sheppie, brandishing her sword in the Sphinx's face.

"Back off! We don't want to hurt you!" she yelled as the creature rose to his full height, towering over them. She hoped she sounded braver than she felt. The Sphinx was huge and powerful and no doubt absolutely deadly!

The appalling creature's wings spread wide, blotting out half the sky as he lifted off the ground and hung menacingly above them, snarling and roaring.

"We're not here to harm you!" shouted Trey, but the Sphinx's great mouth only gaped wider, his huge throat like a red cavern lined with dagger teeth.

Suddenly, the Sphinx curled his wings and plunged down at them, his paws swiping, huge claws scything the air.

Sam and Trey raised their weapons. Sam's sword glanced off a raking claw with a *clang*. Shock waves ran down her arms as she was sent spinning to the ground. Trey's axe was beaten aside and he had to dive head first into the sand to save himself.

Sam struggled to her feet, spitting

sand. Sheppie was approaching the Sphinx, her arms raised. "Hear me! I am Shep—"

The creature's paw struck the princess, knocking the breath out of her, sending her tumbling.

"Hey! Stop that!" howled Sam, charging the Sphinx, her sword shining brightly as she swung at the creature's injured paw.

The Sphinx rose again, lifting out of range, hissing and spitting, his yellow eyes blazing with rage.

"You want a piece of me?" Sam yelled. "Bring it on!"

"Sam, no!" Trey was on his feet again. "We have to get out of here!" He stumbled over to Sheppie, helping her up, his fearful eyes on the circling Sphinx.

"We can take him!" shouted Sam.

The Sphinx's wings folded and he dived, his claws stretching out as he hurtled downwards, levelling off at the last second like some kind of precision-guided smart missile skimming the desert . . .

Heading straight for them.

"Uh-oh!"

The three of them ran.

"Cave!" yelled Trey, pointing to a dark crack in the rock face.

Sam could hear the rush of the Sphinx's wings behind her as she raced for cover. She could feel his burning breath on her neck.

Any moment now, they would be run down and crushed.

Sheppie was first into the cave. Sam and Trey scrambled in together through the narrow entrance. They fell, gasping, to the ground.

There was a crashing noise like a wrecking ball hitting the side of a house. The sun was blotted out and the small cave echoed with the noise of scrabbling claws and gnashing teeth.

The injured paw jabbed inside, the claws like great carving knives. Sam shoved Sheppie out of harm's way, but the thrashing paw crashed down on Sam's back, pinning her to the ground, the claws digging into her backpack.

The air was beaten from her lungs

as her sword slipped from her fingers. She fought for breath, but the paw was crushing her into the rock.

"I got you!" Trey yelled as he snatched at Sam's hand, trying to haul her free.

But the pull of the Sphinx was too strong. Sam could feel her hand slipping out of Trey's grip.

So much for saving the world . . . I can't even save myself!

9

A NEW FRIEND?

"No!" Trey shouted as Sam's fingers slid out of his hand. "*Sam!*" He lifted his axe above his head, meaning to bring it down on the Sphinx's paw with all the strength he could muster. But the weapon twisted in his grip, as if manipulated by an invisible hand.

What's happening?!

The axe almost took Trey off his feet as it towed him to the cave's narrow mouth. He clung on grimly as the axe hacked itself into the wall above the entrance, the blade biting into the stone. It was as though his weapon was thinking for itself. *What's it trying to do?* The shard of cut stone dropped, wedging the Sphinx's leg in the entrance.

Sam writhed underneath the paw as the bellowing Sphinx ripped and heaved at his leg, trying to free himself from the cave mouth. "Trey! Get me out!" she yelled.

Trey stared at the wooden shaft that jutted from the blood-matted wound.

The creature must be in terrible pain. Maybe, if I take the spear out...?

Trey flung himself at the paw. He grabbed the snapped-off shaft of the spear in both hands and pulled upwards. The creature let out a fearsome howl as the shaft came loose, sending Trey stumbling backwards.

He saw the Sphinx's leg give a final wrench. The stone wedge broke free and the paw vanished through the entrance. Sam scrambled clear, gasping for breath. Success!

Sheppie ran forward and helped her up.

"Oww!" said Sam, rotating her shoulders. "That wasn't much fun!"

"Now what?" Trey wondered. "We

might be safe in here – but that thing will mash us to a pulp the moment we take a step outside."

Sheppie knelt to peer through the cave entrance. "I am not so sure," she murmured. "Look!"

The cousins crouched beside her and followed her gaze. The Sphinx was still there, but he was lying flat on his belly, his wings folded against his flanks. He was busy licking his injured paw.

"Do you hear that?" said Sam, her voice full of wonder. "He's *purring*!"

A low rumbling sound carried across the air, rising and falling with the creature's breaths.

"Come forth," growled the Sphinx. "I

know why you are here, Chosen Ones. I shall do you no harm."

"You pulled the spear from his paw," Sheppie said in amazement. "You took the pain away. He's going to *help* us!"

The cousins stared at one another. "Seriously?" said Sam. "Are we safe now?"

"Maybe," Trey replied.

"But I stabbed him in the first place," said Sam.

Trey smiled. "It's probably not a great idea to tell him that. Come on – I think we're going to be fine."

Sam led them out of the cave. The great creature stood up, then turned and walked away, huge and magnificent despite the limp from his wounded paw.

His tail twitched and his wing-feathers ruffled in the hot desert breeze. It was difficult to believe that a few moments ago they'd been fighting this creature for their lives.

Shaking her head in delighted disbelief, Sam followed the Sphinx, Trey and Sheppie at her side.

The creature stopped in the middle of the canyon.

"Now what?" hissed Trey.

"Watch!" whispered Sam.

The Sphinx extended one paw – but not to attack. He scratched at the sand ...

"He's digging for something," murmured Sam.

Trey moved closer as the Sphinx

continued to dig. He heard the raw scrape of claws on stone. Peering down, he saw a long slab of stone being revealed. Hieroglyphs were carved into the surface, timeworn and hard to make out.

Trey frowned, taking another step closer. What was the Sphinx unearthing? What did the ancient writing mean?

The Sphinx raised his forepaw high to swipe at the ground one last time, creating a swirling storm of sand. Now, the slab was completely revealed . . .

Four holes, in the exact formation of a giant feline paw, were cut into the stone. The Sphinx reached down, claws extended. The points of the claws fitted perfectly into the holes, and when the Sphinx pressed down, a low rumbling, grating sound echoed through the canyon. The ground beneath their feet began to vibrate.

The Sphinx drew his paw back as, very slowly, the stone rose from one end, as though pivoting on hidden hinges. Trey leaned closer.

Stone steps descended into pitch darkness. Unlit torches jutted from the walls that ran down both sides of the steep stairway.

Sam swallowed hard. "I think we're going to need some light down there," she said uneasily as she stared into the gloomy stairwell.

As though in response to her words, the Sphinx reached out, scratching his claws down the underside of the stone lid. Sparks flew downwards, sizzling in the uppermost torches.

A moment later, a tongue of flame licked up from one of the torches and another caught alight. Then the next torch down on both sides burst into fire. The flames leapt from torch to torch, dancing along the shaft until the whole plunging stairway was lit up.

"Nice one, Mr Sphinx," Sam said, tightening her grip on her sword. She looked at Trey and Sheppie. "I guess we should check out the basement now?"

Trey nodded, his axe ready in his

hand. This stairway must lead to Horos-Aha's tomb. Now, all they had to do was find the second piece of the Warrior's Shield and prove that they really were the Chosen Ones.

10

ALL WHO ENTER HOROS-AHA'S TOMB MUST DIE!

The narrow walls of the long stairway were covered in carvings. There were rows of marching soldiers. People working in fields or carrying heavy loads. Men in strange, curved, stylised boats.

Hundreds of figures with spears and shields and swords.

"All this work, and no one to see it," murmured Sam as they descended. She was trying to distract herself from how small and dark the space was. *It's fine. It's absolutely fine. I can do this.*

"They are for the gods," said Sheppie, gazing at the engravings.

Trey pointed to an image of a jackal-headed figure weighing something on a large set of scales while a man looked on. He'd seen this during his research. "That's Anubis weighing someone's heart," he murmured. "If the heart was light, you'd get to enter the afterlife in one piece – if it was heavy, you got eaten by a crocodile god."

"Lovely," said Sam with a shudder.

"All these images have great meaning," Sheppie added. "My people carve them to please the gods and to help the dead on their journey into the afterlife."

The stairs came to an end. Sam turned to look back – the exit was now a small blue square far above them, no bigger than a Post-it note. She could just make out the silhouette of the Sphinx's head against the sky. A long corridor stretched away in front of them, lit by flickering torches. Sam looked at Trey, hoping a joke might lighten the mood:

"If mummies start coming alive, I'm out of here, OK?"

"Deal," said Trey with a grim smile.

She knew neither of them meant it.

Sam took a deep breath and stepped forward.

We're in an ancient Egyptian tomb. What can possibly go wrong?

With a sharp, scraping sound, the stone beneath her foot sank. She pulled back in alarm . . .

Nothing more happened.

She turned, grinning anxiously at the others. "Phew! For a moment there, I thought it was going to be like some horror movie – you know? With booby traps and—"

A low grinding noise sounded from above them.

They all looked upwards.

"What's that?" asked Trey.

"We have angered the gods by coming here," muttered Sheppie. "We should go back."

"We can't," Sam reminded her. "We're here on a mission. Remember?"

The harsh grind of stone got louder, closer. Sand dribbled down from cracks in the ceiling.

"It's dropping!" gasped Trey. "See that? A whole section of the ceiling is coming down."

Sam saw. A block about two metres square was very slowly dropping towards them. A knot twisted in her stomach. This was bad. This was so very bad.

"I have heard tales of such things," said Sheppie, her voice trembling. "Traps to deter grave robbers. The stone will block the way out. We shall join the dead ... for ever."

"Not if we get our act together," Sam said. "Look how slowly it's coming down. Move it, guys. We have to be in and out before that oversized Lego block seals us in."

She turned and sprinted wildly along the corridor, hearing the echoing thud of the others running along behind her. She felt less hemmed in than she'd expected. *That's what running for your life will do!* Stone statues lined the walls: some in niches, no bigger than dolls; others as tall as Sam; all wearing headdresses, staring with malevolent eyes.

She didn't like the way the flickering

torchlight made their eyes look like they were following her as she ran.

Behind the statues, column after column of hieroglyphs stretched from the floor to the ceiling.

They came to a pair of stone doors, blocking the way ahead.

Sam shoved against them with her shoulder. To her surprise they edged inwards. "I was expecting it to be more difficult than this."

"I guess this is a perk of destiny, huh?" said Trey, helping her to ease the heavy doors further open. They pushed through into a long chamber that stretched away sideways. One closed door stood opposite them – and there was another at the far end of the room.

Sam turned in a hasty circle. There were no creepy-looking statues in here, but there was something distinctly unsettling about the carvings that ran around the walls. They were of rows of animal-headed people, all seated on stone chairs, some of them gripping actual flaming torches, and all staring out like grim-looking judges.

"I fear this chamber," Sheppie said in a very small voice.

Sam tightened her grip on her sword and took a deep breath, forcing her fear to stay where it belonged – deep down.

"Which door?" she said, moving into the room. "Quickly!"

"That one," Trey said, pointing to the first door. Sam flung herself across the room and slammed her shoulder into it.

"Owww!" She reeled back, pain lancing through her arm and shoulders. The door was solid.

"The writing!" cried Sheppie, pointing above the door. "It says, 'This is the door to the underworld.' ... It cannot be opened by living people. It is for the souls of the dead."

"Well, that's just marvellous, isn't it?" hissed Sam, rubbing her shoulder as she ran down to the other door. "Fake doors, now!"

"Watch out!" Trey's voice rang out a moment before an echoing crash reverberated through the chamber, shaking the floor under Sam's feet. She spun around, a sudden dread exploding in her mind. The doors they'd come through had slammed shut.

Trey leapt at them, but there were no handles on the inside. He scrabbled frantically at the crack where the doors met, but he couldn't get his fingers in.

Sam's fear was beginning to climb back up from deep down.

There's no way back! We're trapped!

"Keep going!" Trey shouted to Sam, as he worked the head of his axe into the narrow slit, struggling to get the fine blade between the tight lips of stone.

Sam charged towards the far door. Maybe she could force herself through. She was almost there when she felt the floor move under her feet. She heard a low, rasping, scraping noise that seemed to be coming from everywhere at once.

For a split second Sam thought her mind was playing tricks on her. Then the floor began to tilt sideways as the noise increased. The door ahead of her turned at an angle.

The next thing Sam knew, she crashed on to her back against stone slabs. She was slithering downwards. The floor had become as steep as a roof. Shadows leapt and writhed as the flames of the torches flared.

The entire chamber was turning over. Trey gave an "Ooof!" as he crashed to his hands and knees beside Sheppie.

The princess was quietly moaning as she slid helplessly around.

Sam twisted as she slid down the steep incline so that she would hit the wall feet first.

She glanced back. Sheppie was tumbling headlong, and Trey was splayed against the doors as the chamber tipped on to its side, the sharp edge of his axe scraping along the stone in a shower of orange sparks.

Boom!

The whole chamber trembled like an earthquake had hit it. The wall had become the floor. Sam stumbled across the uneven surfaces of the carved shapes beneath her, almost twisting her ankle on the ridges and hollows of the animal-

headed creatures. She zigzagged to avoid the licking fire from the torches.

Must get to the door!

She staggered forward, but she'd only taken two steps when the grinding noise rose to a shriek and the chamber began to tip again, quicker this time. Sam hardly had time to drop to the ground before she found herself skimming on her back towards the ceiling.

Shadows whirled. Some of the torches went out. A sudden dreadful darkness began to invade the room. But as the chamber became still again – entirely upside down now – Sam gathered her wits and flung herself at the door. The upside-down lintel of the door was just over waist height. She heaved herself up on to it. The door was decorated in a kind of chessboard pattern – and in each square was a carved figure.

Sam hammered the hilt of her sword against the inverted door. "Open up!" she yelled. She looked over her shoulder at the others. "There's no handle! I don't know what to do!"

Grrrinnnnnnddd.

The chamber turned again. Sam clung on to the sides of the door, jamming her feet against the door frame, refusing to be thrown off as the room rolled over.

Sheppie and Trey were clawing their way towards her.

"Wadjet is the goddess of protection,"

cried Sheppie, pointing a trembling finger at the door.

"So what?" gasped Sam.

"She will help us!"

Sam stared at the figures on the door. "Which one is Wadjet?" she called against the rising grind. The chamber was on the move again. Even faster this time.

"The cobra!" cried Sheppie.

Sam searched the door. Yes! There it was! A rearing cobra with a high crown on its head. She slammed her hand against the square. It shifted under her fingers.

A moment later, the door slid open.

The room was on its side again as Sam clambered desperately through the doorway. She turned, reaching out for the others as they slithered on the revolving surfaces.

Trey pushed Sheppie ahead. Sam managed to grab her hands and haul her to safety.

As the room spun again, Trey came hurtling through the doorway. All three of them crashed to the floor in a tangled heap.

The door slammed shut behind them.

Sam gasped at the sudden stillness and silence.

At least this room is the right way up!

Sam staggered to her feet, aching all over. An unpleasant smell wafted into her nose. Sewers. Sour milk. Rotting meat.

They were in a brightly lit chamber. More of the horrible animal-headed statues lined the walls. A massive granite box stood at the far end of the room.

"That's got to be Horos-Aha's sarcophagus," panted Trey. Sam noticed him wincing in pain as he got to his feet. She helped Sheppie up. Between them and the sarcophagus, the floor was heaped with a crazy assortment of things. Small statues of people and horses and cattle. Stone jars. Caskets filled with gold and jewels. Gold plates and cups. All jumbled up together.

"Do you see the piece of the Warrior's Shield?" asked Trey, looking around. "We have to find it."

"I'm looking," said Sam, as she took a step towards the treasure hoard.

A shrill voice rang out, stopping her like a jolt of electricity.

"All who enter the tomb of Horos-Aha must die!"

"No!" She spun around. "Not *again*!"

The animal-headed statues were not stone – they were more of the Children of Horos! The vile creatures stepped away from the walls, their armour creaking, their eyes glittering with evil. Baboon faces grinned with flesh-ripping fangs. Crocodile jaws gaped. Ferocious lips drew back from panther teeth. Sharp beaks stretched open as thin tongues flickered.

A hawk-headed monster lifted his

spear-arm, his hooked beak wide open, his eyes glistening.

"Did you think to escape us, doomed minions of the Light?" he croaked. "Die now in wretched anguish. The Dark can never be defeated!"

11

BATTLE TO
THE DEATH

The hawk-headed monster flung his spear at Sam, cawing with triumph.

With a sudden burst of speed, Sam twisted, whirling her sword. The blade deflected the spear, sending it clattering against the wall.

The Children of Horos let out howls of animalistic rage.

"Didn't expect us to be tooled up, did you?" yelled Sam. Another spear flew. Again she fended it off with a single sweep of her sword.

Roaring and shrieking and braying and howling, the Children of Horos surged forward. Trey had about half a second to fear for Sam's safety before the first monster loomed above him and Sheppie, gibbering from a wide baboon mouth, its spear poised to strike.

Trey jumped in front of Sheppie and swung the axe. He winced as the razor sharp blade sliced through the creature's wrist and embedded itself in its neck.

There was a scream of rage and then – while Trey was still reeling from the horror of what he'd done – the hideous monster exploded into dust. The armour and the spear tumbled to the ground.

He swung the axe again, gripping it in both hands. A crocodile-headed beast jumped back, hissing. Another with a leopard's head jabbed its spear, but Trey ducked and cut upwards with the amazing axe, chopping the spear in two.

He glanced over to where Sam was being slowly pushed back by several of the monsters at once. She swiped at them with her sword, but she was off balance, stumbling as they crowded in on her.

"Chop their heads off!" Trey yelled.

"Got it!" Sam darted forward, ducking under a spear thrust. She stabbed at the hawk-headed monster's throat. Its croaking scream was cut short by an eruption of fine dust. The armour crumpled.

A stone jar flew past Trey's ear and struck one of the beasts in the face.

"We shall not die, fiend!" he heard Sheppie cry, as she reached for another jar. "It is *your* foul existence that will come to an end."

Way to go, Sheppie!

Another monster leapt forward, thrusting at lightning speed with its spear. Trey only just managed to hurl himself sideways as the spear grazed past his hip. He spun, axe extended. But the monster brought its spear up under Trey's weapon, knocking it away and jolting him backwards.

His feet tangled together and he crashed to the floor, pain burning all down his arm and side. A bird-headed creature stood over him, legs spread, feet on either side of his chest. It let out a terrible screech as it raised the spear in both hands, point downwards, aiming for Trey's heart.

This is it – I'm dead! We've failed.

A rain of stone jars hit the beast. Sheppie was scooping them up from the floor and flinging them like a baseball pitching machine set to max.

The monster threw its arms up,

warding off the bombardment. That was the opening Trey needed. He scrambled to his feet, got a good tight grip on his axe, and swung it at the creature.

The bird head leapt from the shoulders, a look of startled rage in its eyes for a moment before it burst into a fountain of fine grey powder. *They're not even real people*, Trey reassured himself. *They're just things.* Evil, inhuman things that wanted to kill him!

"Trey – take care!" Sheppie's voice was shrill above the howling and roaring of the creatures. Trey twisted around, swinging his axe blindly. A lizard-faced beast towered over him, its long forked tongue flickering, its claws reaching for him.

Swipe! Swipe!

The creature fell back as Trey advanced, swinging his axe in wide arcs. Its spear darted at Trey's face. He jerked his head sideways as the blade almost took out his eye. He could feel his strength ebbing. His shoulders ached and there was a pain like molten steel shooting through the muscles of his arms.

If I get ... out of this ... I'm going to ... hire a ... personal ... trainer ...

The beast kicked Trey in the side, sending him crashing to the ground, blinded by pain. The magical hilt slipped out of his fingers. He saw the monster rise above him.

And then there was a sudden flare

of dust as heavy pieces of bronze and leather armour came crashing down on him.

"Are you OK?" Sam asked.

He clambered to his feet, shaking off chunks of armour and spitting out dust. "Kind of," he said, gazing around. There were piles of armour scattered over the floor.

The Children of Horos had disappeared.

Sam wiped her arm across her forehead. "I think we got them all."

"I think we did," agreed Trey.

"This is yours." Sheppie picked up the golden hilt. The axe had vanished.

"Thanks." Trey took it. The axe didn't reappear. Maybe they didn't need weapons any more? But Sam still had her sword. *That's a bit odd.*

"I can't see the piece of the Warrior's Shield anywhere," said Sam, staring around the cluttered chamber. She pointed towards the sarcophagus. "What's the bet it's in there? That would be the safest place." She stepped carefully through the scattered treasures. "And the creepiest!" she added with a shudder. "Come on, guys, we can't have much time left before that stone block hits the floor in the first corridor."

Trey still felt dazed and bruised from the battle, but the fact that they had won made the pain bearable. *I guess we're warriors now!*

He and Sam stood either side of the

granite box. The lid came up to their chests. Sheppie was at the foot, her face twisted in anxiety.

As grossed out as I *am by all this, it has to be worse for Sheppie*, Trey thought. *Her people aren't meant to mess with their dead – especially not dead pharaohs!*

Sam got a grip on the thick lid. "On three," she said. "One ... two ... *three!*"

Trey and Sheppie pushed while Sam pulled. The lid moved with a screech that set Trey's teeth on edge.

Sam leapt back as the heavy lid crashed to the floor, breaking in two.

Biting his lip, Trey leaned over the sarcophagus.

His first sight of the mummy of Horos-Aha took his breath away. It was lying out straight and stiff on its back, swaddled in grey bandages, its arms folded over its chest. But it was the face that fascinated and repelled Trey.

No bandages. Just a small, hard skull with white desiccated skin stretched over it. The sunken eyes were closed, the cheekbones and nose as sharp as splintered stone. The mouth was a black slot, lipless ... *Almost grinning*, Trey thought with a shudder.

"Oh, wow!" Sam's voice broke into Trey's thoughts. "Take a look at that!"

She was pointing to the mummy's chest. Trey blinked.

The mummy's thin arms were folded over a quarter-circle of metal ... shiny, grey – *familiar* – metal.

"The Warrior's Shield!" gasped Sam. "How great is that?"

She reached into the sarcophagus and prized the quarter-shield out of the mummy's grip.

"Thank you, Mr Horos-Aha. I'll take that if you don't mind."

Trey's heart almost stopped as the

mummy's eyes snapped open. Its lipless mouth gaped as it unleashed a scream of rage. Its hands rose, snatching at the piece of shield, ripping it out of Sam's fingers.

"It is under an evil spell!" yelled Sheppie, as the mummy writhed in the sarcophagus. "You must stab it through the heart to destroy it!"

Sam lifted her sword, but the mummy surged upwards, one arm smashing her sword-hand aside, knocking the hilt out of her fingers. As it spun through the air, the blade vanished. The silver hilt crashed to the floor.

"The Warrior's Shield is mine to protect!" The mummy spoke in a terrible, wheezing voice. "You shall not take it from me. The Dark will not allow it!"

One skeletal hand lifted off the quarter-shield, snatching at Sam's neck, the fingers closing around her throat. The mummy squeezed as Sam struggled to get free. Trey could see his cousin fighting for breath. She couldn't be strangled – not after everything they'd been through!

Sheppie threw herself into the heaped treasures, flinging things aside. "The magical sword!" she gasped. "It has to be here somewhere!"

Trey stared for a moment at his own useless hilt, then lunged across the sarcophagus, snatching at the mummy's bandages, trying to pull it off Sam.

But the ancient wrappings came away in his fingers, revealing a horrible, emaciated body beneath. Taut yellow skin, as thin as paper over brittle bones.

Sam's hands had hold of the mummy's wrist, trying to prize its fingers away from her throat. Her eyes bulged. Trey could see she only had seconds to live – and his hilt was useless!

No! Wait! Idiot!

He took a deep breath and held the hilt out, aiming it at the mummy's back. "Choose weapon!" he shouted.

A long, thin blade, fine as a rapier, shot out, stabbing into the mummy's dried-up body. The mummy jerked, its back arching. One hand groped behind itself. The fleshless head twisted, the mouth gaping silently.

The black eyes saw Trey. The hand reached for his throat.

As Trey watched in horror, the mummy collapsed in on itself. The head rolled from the shoulders, the bandages unravelling, the fingers falling to pieces and the bones clattering down into the sarcophagus.

There was a sound like a sigh as dust settled. A strange silence filled the chamber. Sam was massaging her throat, swallowing hard, looking shocked.

"We did it," said Trey.

Sam nodded, reaching into the sarcophagus and picking up the shield quarter.

"I found your weapon!" said Sheppie, lifting the silver hilt from among the treasures.

"Thanks," said Sam, taking it from her. "Now let's hope we can make it out of here in time."

The door that had led them into the burial chamber had the same chessboard patterns on its back. Sheppie touched the image of Wadjet and the door slid open.

The room beyond was still now, and dark. The only light came from beyond the open doors at the far end. They ran the length of the room, turning into the corridor.

There, they heard the ominous grating of descending stone. They raced at full pelt towards the exit.

The stone block was almost at the ground now.

They shoved Sheppie through first, flat on her stomach. Trey and Sam followed right behind, the stone scraping their backs as they slithered on their bellies.

"Ow!" gasped Sam. "I'm stuck!"

Trey wriggled over to her. It was the backpack! He yanked at the straps, trying to pull it off her shoulders. His cousin twisted and turned, fighting wildly, but the huge stone block pressed down harder.

Trey stared into her frightened eyes.

She was trapped and there was no way for him to help her.

12

FLYING HOME

As Sam struggled to move forward under the crushing weight of the stone, she felt the shoulder straps of the backpack biting savagely into her skin.

She kicked, digging the toes of her shoes into the ground for leverage.

No way! Not when we're this close to escaping!

Trey was clawing at her, right by her side. Sheppie's arms reached back under the stone, searching for a grip.

"Try to get at the buckle," Sam gasped, hardly able to breathe now.

Trey's fingers scrabbled and Sam felt one of the straps loosen. The other one was out of his reach. She would have to release that herself. She was able to twist and wriggle with her arm, shrugging off the strap that Trey had slackened. She wormed her arm under herself, straining to get her fingers to the other shoulder strap.

All she could hear was the relentless grinding of descending stone. When she let out her breath, the weight bore down on her so much that she could not draw another. Her fingers found the buckle. Moaning from the pain in her chest, she just managed to flick the plastic catch open.

"Pull it off me!" she cried.

Trey wrenched at the backpack. For a terrible moment Sam thought it was too late. But then she felt the bag moving. She could hear Trey panting as he strained to drag the bag off her shoulders.

Suddenly the ground beneath her shook, sending a rumble through Sam's body. She felt the pressure on her back ease. She scrabbled forward as Trey flung the bag out to where Sheppie was waiting to grab it.

Sam and Trey slithered out from

under the stone. There was a dull, heavy thud as the massive block hit the ground.

Breathing hard, Sam sat up, massaging her aching ribs. "That was close!" she breathed.

"Way too close," agreed Trey.

Sheppie stared up the long stairway that led back to the desert. "The Sphinx beat his paw upon the ground," she said in awe. "It halted the stone for a moment. He saved you!"

"Way to go, Sphinxie!" gasped Sam.

"Let's go thank him," said Trey.

They scrambled up the stairs. Warm air beat down on them. Sam's head popped up into the fading daylight. The Sphinx was standing close by. His eyes lit up when he saw them emerge. He reared up on to his haunches, pawing the air and taking flight, flapping his mighty wings as he let out a roar of jubilation that almost blasted Sam off her feet.

He came crashing down on to his paws again, joy spreading across his half-human face, his yellow eyes shining as he faced them.

"Four hundred years of servitude to Horos-Aha . . . " he said. "And now, the spell is broken." He bowed his huge head. "Thank you."

"I was just going to say the same," grinned Sam, looking up into his velvet face. "What now for you?"

"I will go home," said the Sphinx.

His eyes brimmed with joyful tears as he gazed into the sky. "Into the deep desert, to be with my people."

Trey looked anxiously at the Sphinx. "The thing is, we need to get the piece of the Warrior's Shield back to our own time, but we can't just abandon Sheppie out here in the middle of nowhere."

"Our horses are gone," Sheppie said mournfully. "And Memphis is far away."

The Sphinx folded his legs beneath him, lying down on his front. "Climb upon my back," he said. "I shall take you closer to your city."

"Can we have a ride, too?" asked Sam.

"Indeed." A look of regret came over the Sphinx's face. "A raging thirst drove me to the river last night.

I did not wish the humans harm."

"We get that," Sam said as she, Trey and Sheppie clambered up on to the Sphinx's enormous shoulders. Sam could feel the warmth of the great creature under her, and as the Sphinx began to purr, the vibrations travelled right through her body.

She clutched clumps of fur between her hands as his massive wings spread on either side of them. There was a sudden surge, a rush of air, a feeling like she'd left her stomach down in the sand, and they were airborne!

"Wheee-hooo!" yelled Sam as the Sphinx climbed higher.

"What's going on over there?" asked Trey, pointing into the south.

Sam turned her head. The far southern horizon was banded with heavy cloud. Tier after tier of deep, dark clouds hugged the land. As she watched, forked lightning snaked down, thin as white thread.

"The rains have come!" laughed Sheppie, clapping her hands. "At last!"

"That's excellent!" Trey looked at Sam. "We should be getting back."

She reached into her backpack and brought out the Heart of Light.

"What is that?" Sheppie asked.

"Our way home," said Sam. She gave the startled princess a hug. "Thanks for everything. I'll miss you."

"I do not understand," said Sheppie.

"We're going to kind of ... *vanish*, OK?"

said Trey. "Don't worry. It's all good." He fished in his pocket and handed her the folded piece of paper with the photo of the Great Sphinx on it. "You might want to show this to your dad. There's a big chunk of rock out near the pyramids that would make an awesome statue!"

"Thank you," said Sheppie, taking the paper. "I will do that."

"Mr Sphinx?" called Sam against the whirl of the wind in her ears. "I hope you get home safely."

"Farewell, Chosen Ones," came the rumbling reply.

Sam and Trey held the Heart of Light between them.

"Bye," Sam said to Sheppie. Then she turned to her cousin. "Ready?"

Trey nodded.

They snapped the disc.

There was a flash of blue-white light and a crack like sudden thunder . . .

. . . and Sam and Trey came tumbling into the basement in New England as though they'd dropped through a hole in the ceiling.

"Oww!" said Sam, picking herself up.

Trey got to his feet with a few groans.

Michael was standing by the wall, watching them with his strange silver eyes. "Were you successful, Chosen Ones?" he asked.

"You bet!" said Sam, swinging her half-ruined backpack off her shoulder and pulling out the quarter-shield. "You'll never believe the fights we had to get this."

A smile brightened Michael's severe face. "The Dark's minions are no match for the Light's Chosen Ones," he said. "Place the piece of the shield with the one from Ancient Greece."

Trey fetched the first part of the Warrior's Shield from inside a box hidden under a bench.

"We found these as well," said Sam, taking out her silver hilt. "Trey has a gold one. They're totally amazing! We'd have been toast without them."

Michael nodded. "Did I not say weapons would come to you if you were worthy?"

"We are *so* worthy …" Sam said, before grimacing, "… and so *tired*."

Trey lay the shield quarter on the ground and Sam knelt at his side, carefully placing the second part next to it.

"See that?" Sam murmured, pointing. Etched into the face of the second quarter of the shield was a picture of the Sphinx, wings spread in flight, claws reaching forward. The first quarter carried the engraved image of Medusa.

The two pieces of the shield began to vibrate. Sam heard a soft humming sound. Then the two pieces jumped together and fused with a burst of electric light.

"Amazing!" said Sam, looking up at

Michael, who was standing silently over them.

"Where's the third piece?" asked Trey, as Sam tucked the half-shield back into the box.

"In Ancient China," said Michael. "Go and rest now – tomorrow's task will come soon enough."

The cousins headed for the stairs.

Sam turned to say goodbye to Michael, but the Lord of Light was already gone.

"I'll tell you something weird," said Trey, at the head of the stairs. "Do you realise that if we hadn't taken that picture of the Great Sphinx back with us, the statue might not have been made in the first place?"

Sam stared up at him. "Huh?"

Trey's eyes glowed. "We asked Sheppie to show the picture to her dad, Khafre, and he went on to build the statue," he said eagerly. "At least, I assume he did. And if he hadn't built the statue, we wouldn't have had the picture in the first place. It's a temporal paradox, see what I mean?"

"You're making my head hurt," growled Sam. "Let's get out of here. I'm starving, and I need a shower!"

She gave Trey a hefty shove and the two of them burst out through the basement door and into the ordinary daylight of Trey's home. Their next adventure could wait. For now . . .

ARE YOU AN EGYPTIAN NERD?

A lot of Sam and Trey's latest adventure was influenced by real myths that you can read about online, or in your local library.

SAM: At least the books in the library won't be written in hieroglyphics.

TREY: I still can't believe I had you going at Ardeth Bey's house. Did you really think I could read the symbols?

SAM: That's the last time I . . .

Um, why don't we just push on with our multiple choice quiz? Brains at the ready!

THE EGYPT EXAM

QUESTION ONE

During the mummification process all internal organs were removed from a body. The brains were taken out by:

A. A special golden syringe that sucked them out through the ears

B. A long hook that pulled them out through the nose

C. A ceremonial spoon that scooped them out via the eye-sockets

---

TREY: They all sound nasty.

The answer is . . .

B: The book, I'm afraid!

SAM: That's one situation where I'd be grateful to be dead.

QUESTION TWO

The original Memphis was in Egypt, but there is also a town called Memphis in America. In which state can it be found?

A. Tennessee

B. New York

C. Florida

SAM: Trey, you're American – you know this, right?

TREY: Of course. It's actually quite easy . . .

Answer:

SAM: Did you know that?

TREY: Erm . . .

QUESTION THREE

In order to gain entrance to the afterlife, a person had to have their heart weighed by Anubis on a set of large scales. What was the weight of the heart measured against?

A. A grain of sand

B. A snowflake

C. A feather

Answer:

C: *A feather.*

SAM: Anubis was the "Guardian of the Scales," and if the deceased person's heart was heavier than an ostrich feather (said to symbolise truth) then that person was deemed unworthy of entering the afterlife.

TREY: Right. And then they would be fed to Ammit, the Devourer of the Dead.

SAM: Nice. Not!

QUESTION FOUR

Shepsetkau had at least twelve brothers and three sisters. They also had tricky names. Which one of these was one of Sheppie's sisters?

A. *Rekhetre*

B. *Ankhmare*

C. *Iunre*

Answer:

A: Rekhetre. The other two were her brothers.

SAM: If they were as chatty as Sheppie, I bet it was a nightmare round their house!

QUESTION FIVE

Hor-Aha, or Horos-Aha, was a pharaoh of the First Dynasty in Ancient Egypt. What are the rough dates we're indicating when we refer to Ancient Egypt?

> A. 5000 BC to 125 AD
>
> B. 3200 BC to 30 BC
>
> C. 3700 BC to 619 AD

TREY: Whatever the answer is, that's a significant era.

SAM: I can't even work out how many lifetimes that would equal.

> Answer:
>
> B: The civilization we talk about as Ancient Egypt lasted from about 3200 BC (the first pharaoh is called "Scorpion 1" because all that is currently known about him is that he had a scorpion engraved on his tomb) to 30 BC and Ptolemy

15th, the infant son of Cleopatra who lost his throne when the Roman Empire conquered Egypt.

TREY: That's over three thousand years! Our civilisation would need to survive another thousand years just to catch up with them!

SAM: You're just showing off now!

QUESTION SIX

The Greek word "sphingo" is believed by some scholars to be the origin of the word "sphinx," but what is its meaning?

A. To squeeze, or tighten up

B. To fly on broad wings

C. To rampage through the desert

SAM: Tough one. Our sphinx-friend kind of
   did all three!

Answer:

A: To squeeze or tighten up.

TREY: I guess it might be because the sphinx
   is part lion, and lions kill their prey by biting
   the throat then squeezing or tightening
   their grip till the animal suffocates.

Correct. But others think it is a Greek
corruption of the Egyptian word "shese-
pankh" – meaning "living image".

SAM: I prefer the lion one! The sphinx had
   different names in different cultures. In
   Egypt it was called "Abu al-Haul" – which,

we know now, means "the terrible one." In South India it was called the "Purushamriga" ("man-beast"), and in Sri Lanka, it was known as "Narasimha" ("man-cat"). In Thailand, it was called "Norasingh," while in Burma, it was referred to by the name "Manussiha" (both meant "man-lion").

TREY: Now who's showing off?

SAM: Over the page is one more question, which you can answer for a chance to win some special Myth Raiders goodies. Good luck, and be thankful you're not answering this question in Ancient Egypt. Get it wrong, and you'd be eaten by the sphinx . . . So they say!

TREY: Yeah, but they also say that, get it

right and the sphinx would be freed from having to kill any more people. Sounds like it could be a risk worth taking!

Sam and Trey succeeded in their adventure because they knew their history. Will they know enough for next time? Let's hope they're prepared for the next challenge ...

COMPETITION TIME!

There are many versions of the Riddle of the Sphinx, and the most famous is:
"What is that which in the morning goes upon four feet; upon two feet in the afternoon; and in the evening upon three?"

A. Man

B. A dog

C. A sphinx with a sore paw

To enter the competition go to
www.mythraiders.co.uk
and fill in your details.

ABOUT THE AUTHOR

A. J. Hunter is the pen name for two authors, Allan and James, who bonded over their shared love of mythical creatures. After poring over their history books and trawling through the Internet, Myth Raiders was born! When they're not thinking up new adventures for Sam and Trey, they can usually be found indulging one of their many interests, such as practising kung fu, growing beards, writing fantasy novels for Young Adults, helping develop apps and selling flowers in Covent Garden market. But which hobby belongs to which author? Only A. J. Hunter knows the answer to that . . .